Ring of Calasia

A Raymond Ferriss Adventure

Eric Kercher

Paper and Sword, LLC

First edition 2024

From the Author

There are days when we all need an escape from a terrible job, a terrible day, or a terrible life.

Join my newsletter and get an escape from the real world, stories, and lore designed to entertain and delight.

You'll also get *Stories from the Deep*, an exclusive, unpublished anthology chock full of extra epilogues, short stories, and lore from the Patmos Sea Fantasy Adventure Series.

Join now at erickercher.com.

Enjoy the book.

-Eric Kercher

Introduction

Raymond Ferriss first enters the stage as a washed-up adventurer in *Architect's Prize*. He acts as a guide to a young man with little in the way of street smarts and ends up being a good friend and a great mentor.

During that book, and even long after the subsequent series was finished, I found myself returning to the question of where Raymond came from. What was it that he did, what kind of adventures did he have to make him so weary of the world and jaded?

What follows in these pages isn't a full account of his life, but mere glimpses. At various times you catch a glimpse of something that affected him or was so instrumental in the shaping of his character, that it completely changed him.

Beware, if you want answers to questions, you will find little. In fact, you may have more questions raised than answered. Whatever the case, enjoy the treasure seeker at the beginning of his life, and during the prime.

Fair Winds,

Eric Kercher

1

To the Depths

The suit stretched and conformed to his body, slithering on like a wet blanket that clung too tight.

"This is the worst part." Raymond grimaced as he hauled up the helmet, squeezing in his head and setting it on his shoulders. His body was off weight, and he nearly fell over.

With it came the stale, sweaty smell of rubber, aged a thousand times through a thousand dives.

He itched to get out of it, the oppressive helmet too small compared to the freedom of the outside world.

"The things I do for treasure," he said. His companions responded, but all he could hear was a faint warble through the metal, glass, and other substances that made up the helmet.

A sudden rogue wave made him clutch the railing, stabbed with a splinter that went into his left hand.

He tried to look at it, bringing it in front of his face, but the haze of the glass was too much and his breath fogged it.

He waved his hand around, an imitation of help as much as he could, and the first mate, Bill, pulled it out with rough, calloused hands.

They were laughing at him, but he would see who would be laughing soon enough.

At last they handed him the speargun, and he was ready. Pulling the heavy boots, he stomped to the edge of the ship, clipping the speargun to his belt. It dangled at his side, a reassuring weight.

The water was turquoise clear and fairly calm, not a white-cap anywhere. Sunlight reflected off the water, scattering in the slight waves that were too round to be waves.

He took a deep breath, licked his salty lips, and then stepped off.

The world dropped, then stopped, then he was falling slower as the water rushed over his helmet and sent him to a different world altogether.

The weight of his suit and his boots pulled him down, sucking and bubbling through the clear water.

His heart beat and that familiar bubbly sensation returned to his stomach, the not quite excitement mixed with fear he had felt many times before.

Oh, how he hungered for it and enjoyed every second of it.

But there was work to be done, and it wouldn't find itself.

His feet contacted the sea floor, spearing him in the sandy bottom. With great resistance, he pulled them free, still sinking slightly.

Raymond stopped. He let himself acclimate to the coolness of the water and observe his surroundings.

What had been dead and similar, a desert of blue everywhere around them, had turned into a forest and explosion of colors.

Fish swam by in every color of the rainbow. Striped, spotted, solid, they frolicked and played, swam and flashed in the poor light that trickled down from above.

Urchins and sea cucumbers dotted the sea floor, with mollusks and crabs that skittered away from him, then came back to see what he was.

Forward, he went, tugging on the hose that ran to the surface, glad it was solid. That was all that connected him to life, and the salty air of the sea above.

"Do you see it?" The voice crackled in his ear, startling him. Raymond jumped, cursed, then replied.

"I'll never get used to that. No, not yet. I'm on the bottom now."

"Get to it." Raymond shook his head, biting back what he really wanted to say to the gruff voice.

The Captain was being well compensated for his time, he should have been more grateful. It wasn't Raymond's fault this place was within the territorial waters of Waverly.

And it wasn't his fault they looked down on what they called looters, killing them on site.

They'd have to catch us first, and we've got one of the fastest ships this side of the Shark's Teeth.

Instead, Raymond grumbled and walked, scattering the too-curious crabs and fish.

It was slow going, the sea dragged at his legs when he lifted them and pulled at him with the current when he wasn't.

The ground sloped down. They had drifted more than he thought, or he had been given the wrong information.

He was starting to wonder when up ahead he thought he saw it in the gathered gloom where the sun refused to go.

Raymond squinted, focused on the point, then saw it again.

Jagged and sharp, the broken mast was the only landmark of the wreckage that he could see.

He smiled. "I've got a sight of it."

"Keep your eyes open. I don't like this place."

"You and your superstitions. Captain, we haven't seen any of your ghosts and we won't." But there was a creeping feeling down the back of his neck that belied his confidence.

"Don't be foolish. The spirits refuse to be mocked."

"I'm more worried about sharks than anything else," Raymond said. Sweat trickled down his eyebrows, despite the cool of the sea. He flexed his hand, trying to get the feeling back in them. His helmet was stuffy, but at least he could see underwater.

"You've been down half an hour. Hurry up." That was the end of the conversation in the Captain's mind, and Raymond didn't mind either.

He grumbled a little, then kept walking. It was getting dark, so much so he could barely see his hands when he brought them up.

But he kept the mast in view, ever going toward it.

The sea floor was sloping faster now, and his boots slipped in the sand.

For the first time on the journey, Raymond was afraid of what he was going to find. Not ghosts, but something else was brooding, pressing on him and he couldn't figure out what.

Had Sella given him bad information? Fed him dung so that he would choke on it? He wouldn't put it past her, vengeful woman.

But that had been a long time ago, and she was more likely to profit handsomely in the endeavor than he was.

No, he trusted her information, if not her.

All of this he thought of to distract himself from that strange feeling in the pit of his stomach.

Suddenly, he felt a jerk on his air hose.

"What is it?" he asked.

"Trouble down there?" a voice came back. Not the Captain's, Parsee, he thought.

"You pulled on my hose."

There was a pause. "Not us."

Raymond looked up, but couldn't see very well, so he leaned back and twisted, aiming the viewing window of his helmet at the faint outline of his hose in the dim light of the sun.

A dark shape touched it again, jerking his head enough to make him feel it.

Raymond cursed.

"What is it?"

"Shark." He saw more shapes. "Sharks."

"We can't see them."

Raymond stomped his feet, thinking. If he activated his light now it might attract them.

But the water was too dark and murky to continue without it.

"Kill them if you can. Time to take a gamble." Raymond reached down, spun the lock, and shook. The sharks played with his air hose again, and he wished they would go away.

At first, he thought it failed. He took a deep breath, then smiled when the glow came. Like a welcome sunrise after a stormy night, it blossomed orange and red, then a stronger yellow beam illuminated the sandy floor below.

He walked faster, glad that the suit was lighter under water, playing his beam along the wreckage.

It was massive, blackened with age and barnacle growth. The prow and stern were both pointing up, a giant crack running down the middle.

There had to be some sort of sunken valley for it to be up like that, and sure enough, he saw what looked like a giant crack running up and under the hull. The two sides of the ship had wedged themselves together.

Another jerk on his air line reminded him not to dawdle, and while he crossed the remaining yards to the wreck, he wondered how he was going to get in.

Or get out.

But that was a problem for the future, and right now he had to get into the shelter because, sure enough, he had managed to attract the attention of at least one of the sharks.

It swam into his beam, powerful tail sending a wave that almost pushed him back. This one was big, far bigger than most, and turned around to come at the light.

Mouth agape, the rows of teeth glinted off his light and Raymond waited until the last second to dive aside, punching it with the speargun.

He was buffeted and hit by the tail or something else he didn't know, and the light beam jerked wildly in the dark.

Dirt and mud from the bottom kicked up, making his light almost unusable, and while he still had the chance, Raymond tried to run in his suit to the wreck.

It was awkward, and he could hardly bring his feet up with the rubber constricting his motions. He was gasping for air after a few steps, lungs burning and heart pounding.

His eyes sought some form of refuge before him in the swirl of mud and darkness, and he thought he saw an opening.

Raymond dove aside, clipped by another shark attack, falling face first into the seabed.

This wasn't good.

He scrambled, fighting the weight of his suit, until he was able to get back up. The opening was still there, shining from the beam of light like a scene from heaven.

To it, Raymond ran.

He swung his head around as he did, but he seemed to be alone.

Finally, he reached the opening on the stern, a hole punched into it the size of a man.

He fit into it, just barely, and squeezed inside, careful to keep his air hose from being crushed or split.

"What's going on down there?" For the first time, Raymond registered the voice of the Captain in his ear. It had been squawking the whole time.

"Nothing," Raymond said, gasping and staring out of the hull of the ship. The sharks circled out there, playing in the beam of his light. "Just some playful fish."

"It sounded worse than that."

"I'm sure it did. I made it inside, I'll be checking it out for the next few minutes. In peace, I might add."

There was a grumble, then silence.

He caught his breath, staring at the sharks and wondering how he was going to get out of this.

That's a problem for the future, he said to himself, then turned his attention to the ship.

It was a wreck. The hole he had come through continued into the ship, getting progressively smaller but with the same clean lines.

Raymond felt the edge of the wood. It was spongy, but still sharp after all these years, a few splinters pushed back into the ship.

This was a puncture wound, and far below the waterline. He knew what had made that but couldn't believe it.

The whole ship was tilted, and he found himself at a choice between uphill and downhill. He stepped through the puncture into another corridor, this one seemed to go far, and entered it.

He started uphill at first, to save the easy part for afterward. The wood bent under his weight, and for a few steps he thought it might give out, but it held and he kept going.

His light played over the hallway, doors hanging askew and a layer of mud around everything. Small fish and crustaceans played in the water and ran from his light, frightened by either it or him.

The suit was starting to itch, and it smelled worse now that his sweat had mixed with the strange rubber smells. Every so often he had to check his air hose, careful to keep enough slack to let him wind it around corners if need be.

This place was a tomb. The remains of bodies floated in rooms that used to be living areas. Most of it had been eaten by the sea or the inhabitants of the sea long ago, but strange artifacts remained.

A silver locket on the floor here, a pair of soles sticking out of the mud there. He found a smashed lantern, the candle eaten out long ago, but the metal intact.

None of it was of any use and not what he was looking for. Closing his eyes, he mapped out where he had been and compared it to the mental image of the ship he had taken from the outside.

He had traversed at least half the ship and was now coming up on the rear. He had gone too far, and he turned back toward the puncture.

Walking past it, he continued until he reached the crack in the hull. No luck, it hadn't been in any of the rooms he checked.

"Time check," said the voice. Parsee again.

"I'm here."

"It's been three hours. Captain says to hurry up, the sun will be down in another two and he'd like to be gone before then."

"I know what I've paid for. I'll take as much time as I want."

Pause.

"It will be hard without air, he says."

Raymond cursed, said a few words he wasn't proud of, then calmed himself. "I'm in the back half of the ship now. This thing is big and hard to get around in."

"Two hours."

Raymond sighed.

So, back to the hunt he went. This time, with a new sense of vigor and deeper into the ship.

The ship groaned and creaked around him, and he kept snagging his air hose on the frames and random planks that had broken free in the decades under water.

Finally, he found a hatch that led down. The ladder looked intact, and he gently put a single foot down on it to test.

It held his weight, so he put his other foot on the next rung.

The rung snapped. He fell, feet slamming against the deck below and knees and shins banging up against the rungs of the ladder as they gave way.

Raymond groaned, now on his back. The light was crushed beneath him, and he shifted off of it to illuminate the darkness he had fallen into.

He expected a response from above, but none came. Swallowing his pride and ignoring the throb in his right knee, he turned.

This part of the ship had taken most of the brunt of time. Bulkheads were crumbling, possessions scattered and littered everywhere, and barnacles grew sharp on every surface.

They reflected his light, and he looked up. On the ceiling they grew in clusters, sharp and menacing. Waiting to slice into his air hose.

He wasn't sure how he was going to get out of this, but took a look around anyway. With luck, there would be something he could use to escape.

Unfortunately, his luck seemed to have run out. He kicked aside a crate, sending something skittering into the darkness. He hoped it was a crab, but it couldn't have been bigger than a house cat.

The open ocean was at the other side of the room, the ravine beneath the ship looming up from beneath them. If he wasn't careful, he would slip down, never to be seen again.

Raymond swallowed and stepped carefully around the debris, looking after his air hose to make sure it wasn't anywhere near those barnacles.

He wondered what poor life choices led him to this line of work, then remembered all the poor life choices he had made.

I guess I deserved it. He was commiserating with himself when he saw something flash, tucked into the bulkhead.

Swinging the light around, he confirmed it was there, between a rotting bulkhead and the great planks of the hull behind.

It looked like an afterthought, a wall put up in hindsight. Or a wall put up to hide something.

A thrill ran through him, from his toes all the way up to the nape of his neck. He couldn't help the smile creep up his face and walked over to it.

There was something back there, if he could get to it. Raymond tugged on the plank, and it crumbled under his touch, dissolving to almost nothing.

The rest of the wall was just as weak, but more intact, and he wrenched it free with a few good tugs, tossing pieces to float around him, and finally, and gracefully, fell to the deck like a butterfly.

It was a chest. His heart beat, his eyes strained under the sweat of exertion, and he knew what it was.

His hands closed on the handle greedily, and he braced one foot against the wall to pull it free.

It came at first, then stuck, they ripped free, making him fall backward.

It fell to the floor with a solid *thunk* and lay there.

A bronze lock tried to keep him out, but a quick kick with his good leg parted it from the chest.

He hesitated, hands on the lid, breathing his own sweat and humid exhaust, and thanked the Lord up above for his luck.

One swift motion opened the chest, revealing the contents.

His eyes widened. "I've found it."

"Repeat, did you say you found it?"

Raymond's hand went into the chest, touched the shimmering jewels that scattered the light into a rainbow of color.

He pushed them aside, going for the flat, dull gray corner that made his heartbeat faster and his eyes go wide with delight.

Jewels shifted aside, and the mark came free with a sucking noise.

There it was, like she said it would be. The key to a fortune, and a powerful artifact from the grave.

He looked up, back at the ladder he had come from.

Now he just had to figure out how to get it out.

2

Suffolk

The sun shone, and the sails fluttered in the breeze, a pennant weaving and snaking along its tall mast.

Raymond peered up at it. "You gonna look at it all day, or are you gonna come aboard?" A sailor, mending lines, worked above him. He had been the one who spoke.

"I'm not sure a bucket like this will take me where I need to go." Raymond slouched, picking at his fingernails.

The sailor snorted. "You can't hide the look in your eyes, no matter what you pretend." He stopped and leaned over, eyes sharp. "For some reason, you want to come on the ship." His eyes narrowed. "Now, why is that?"

The sea breeze brought in the fresh smell of salt, banishing the stench of decay that spread along the docks up and down the bay. Below it was the smell of fish. Fresh, rotting, stale.

"I'd have a word with your master. See where she's going and if I want to take her there."

The sailor studied him, then pointed to the gangplank. "He's in his quarters." He jabbed a knife back toward the stern of the ship.

She was a three masted sloop, low to the waterline with graceful curves that would cut through the water like butter.

Raymond stepped onto the gangplank, rocking with the aftereffects of the waves in the bay. He swallowed, and put out his hands, trying not to peer over into the water.

It swayed ever so gently as he crept across, but then it was done and over with and he was on good, solid deck.

Still rocking, he felt much better, and slung his pack up as it had slipped on his journey across.

He hazarded a glance back to the sailor, who was smiling with amusement at his ways. Raymond scowled and turned to the door beneath the quarterdeck, rapping on it after a mere breath of hesitation.

"Come," a booming, deep voice said. Raymond entered, astonished at the cleanliness at once.

Everything was put in its place. Tacked, pinned, and pegged except for a set of books at the desk beneath the window.

Set over the books was the master, writing and scratching at them. He lowered his big, bushy eyebrows. "What do you want? Can't you see I'm busy?"

Raymond swept off his hat with a simple bow. "Raymond Ferriss, at your service, sir. I wish to see where your ship is headed and inquire as to passage."

"Passage?" The master licked his finger, shuffling through the book. "I've room for two at most, and one of the beds is filled. We're headed to Fjel and the east for trading."

"Picking up goods, I suppose?"

"What business is mine of yours, Mr. Ferriss?"

Raymond paled and held up his hands. This was not going as he planned. "None at all, sir, no offense meant."

"If you plan to ride the *Suffolk* you need to understand something and understand it well." The master stood, raising his substantial figure to its full bulk. "I am the master of this ship and my word is Law. If that's going to be a problem then you can march back out and find another ship to take you."

They were going in the right direction, if not the same destination, and he found an attractive pull to the *Suffolk* for some reason.

"I understand completely," Raymond said, mollified.

"Very good. Now, let's get down to business, shall we?" They haggled over the price, the master getting the upper hand, but in the end Raymond agreed and was booked onto the *Suffolk*, with a departure time at sunrise the day after next.

Raymond wrung his hands. He had wanted to be away earlier, but none of the other ships had been going where he wanted. He suspected the master knew this and was playing him, but there was no getting around it.

He had two days to keep his head down. A seagull crowed above, flying lazy arcs around the ship.

"He didn't scare you away, eh?" the sailor said.

"No, not at all." Raymond realized that he might as well introduce himself since he'd be sharing a small ship with him.

"Isaiah," the sailor said, shaking hands with a grip like iron.

"How long have you been on the *Suffolk*?"

"Years now. Ever since I came to sea, before I was an able seaman and just a greenhorn. She's a real beauty, rode her through storm and fair alike."

"She seems fast."

"Aye, that she is, when trimmed and set in the right manner. She practically races over the waves, skipping like a stone." The man turned his head, checking the docks. "What made you sign up?"

"Oh, she's headed east like me, and I figured one ship is no better than another."

"Everyone's running from something, aren't they?"

Raymond's eyes widened in surprise. "Running?" he spluttered. "Whatever makes you think of that?"

"I've seen 'em before. Light pack, look in your eye. You can't hide it, young one."

A cart trundled by on the docks, a baker hawking his wares of sweet and sour breads. The smell drifted over the docks and up to the deck. "I'm not running from anything."

"Suit yourself," Isaiah said, looking sidelong at him. The conversation turned to other things, the weather, the ship, the journey, but something stuck with him afterward.

Isaiah showed him his quarters, a cramped room with bunks and little else but a light. There were three spots.

"The master said there was one other passenger besides myself, but there are three bunks. Who shares the other?"

"The first mate. He's had it for years. No hammocks below deck for a man like him." Isaiah grinned.

Raymond tested the mattress, harder than a rock, and opened the small locker to the side. Plenty of room for his belongings, he thought.

There wasn't much room to do anything, and Isaiah had to return to his work. That left him with nothing to do and nowhere to go.

Raymond thought about what he could do. Should he stay on the ship and wait until it left?

But he would be on it for weeks, months even. He wouldn't have the chance to leave and see the world like he did now.

He mulled it over, then finally decided he would risk it. He had to go out, see what he could see while he still could.

So he went topside and crossed the gangplank back to the shore, joining the hustle and bustle of work on the docks.

Sailors and dockworkers rushed by, carrying goods, pushing barrels. They trundled past with a dull sound, sometimes things inside them tumbling and swishing around.

Merchants joined the throng, selling their sweet-smelling baked goods or freshly fried fish. They provided some respite from the other smells of manure and waste that permeated the salt air.

Raymond exchanged some of his money for a skewer of meat, biting into its tangy flesh that dribbled juices down his chin. It was spicy, but good and hot still. He ate it while he walked into the city, keeping an eye out.

It was when he walked past the hattery that he decided to change his appearance, purchasing a small hat with a wide brim he could pull down to hide his hair and cover his face. He examined himself in the faded polished plate the hatter used as a mirror.

"That suits you well," the young salesman said. It made Raymond feel good, and he bought it.

He was glad he did, for the afternoon sun was beating down hard now, baking everything in sight of it. A few white clouds rolled far off in the distance as he left the shop.

"Rain, we need rain," an old crone crowed next to him. "Alms for the poor?" She held out a battered cup and rattled it at him.

Raymond said nothing and slid away, and she cursed at him with wild abandon as he did. But soon another caught her interest, and he evaded into the crowd.

He let it take him, not knowing where he was going or caring much either. Men and women pushed and bustled, jostling him up the docks, but eventually the crowd thinned out at a market, spilling him into a side alleyway.

The people kept walking, but Raymond figured it was as good as any place to take a rest. He looked up, letting the sun beat on his face and warm it, glad that he had made it out alive and in one piece.

Behind him, something moved. He whirled around, but it was a cat. It hissed at him, arching his back, then decided he was no threat and turned and stalked away.

The two houses pressed up against each other above, blocking out the light of the sun and casting the alley into darkness. Raymond could see down it, but an uneasy feeling made him rejoin the crowd. It was like eyes were on his back.

Something, or someone, was watching him.

Gone was the free and easy care he'd had earlier, vanished into the ocean breeze. He glanced behind him every so often now, checking to see if he was being followed.

"Young lad, you look as if you could use my wares." A man with a pleated shirt half unbuttoned beckoned to him. Raymond looked around. "Yes, you. Come over and see what I have."

The man picked up a saber and unsheathed it. "The finest steel to keep you safe from dangers in the dark, and the light, mind you." He held it up, traced along the back. "A gentle curve, a graceful sweep."

Raymond walked closer, enticed.

"Or would you prefer a shorter blade?" A dagger was in the man's hand the next instant. "Easy to draw, easy to kill." Raymond hadn't seen him take it out, and then it was gone in a flash. "Easy to conceal."

The merchant spread his arms over his table, the cloth filled with weapons of every kind.

Swords made up the bulk, but they too differed in every way.

"I like this one." Raymond touched a straight blade, with a strong hilt and a polished surface it spoke to him of battle and adventure.

"Ah, a good choice. Kalian steel, the finest in the world." The merchant picked it up. "Thin," he said, tapping its side. It sang with a hum, "but strong." He stuck it in the table point down and flexed it. It bent but didn't break.

Raymond tried not to look impressed. "May I hold it?"

The merchant bowed, turned the sword, and offered it hilt first.

He took it. It was cool at first, the metal sucking the heat from his hand, but it warmed quickly.

Raymond checked the area, waited until it was relatively clear, and gave the sword a few test swings.

It hummed through the air, as if it were cutting it. It felt good, solid but light, strong but supple.

"Good, isn't it?" The merchant wore a smile. "And a bargain at only three hundred crowns."

His stomach dropped into his shoe, and he almost felt like he was going to be sick. Raymond held the thing like a viper now and turned gingerly to return it to the table.

"Do you have anything...else?" he asked.

The merchant produced a set of daggers without hesitation. "A fine array of daggers, at a cheaper price." He named a few, and Raymond's reluctance was palpable but lower.

He tried haggling the price lower, but the merchant refused to budge, going to less impressive and cheaper looking blades instead.

Raymond kept looking at the sword he had picked up, longing to buy it and take it with him. He could see it strapped to his side as he clung to the rigging, sea salt spraying in his face as they rushed over the waves to adventure and glory.

He settled on a plain dagger, with a sheath, because it was all he could afford. After the counting was done, painfully, he handed his pile of treasure over and took the dagger.

"Pleasure doing business with you," the merchant said, and immediately turned to the next person in the street.

Raymond slipped the dagger in his belt, hidden inside his pants, and put his shirt over it. It was cool against his belly, and hard, but comforting.

The feeling of dread he had was lessened now, and he wandered the stalls, careful not to go in any lest he spend more. There was barely enough for the voyage.

Light of afternoon turned to evening, then the sun began to kiss the horizon on its long journey to the night.

Raymond left the market, tired of walking and staying on his feet, and went back to the ship, patting the dagger every once in a while.

The docks were empty now, but the brothels and bars were filled. He walked past them, wondering what it was like inside, until a door opened and a pair of sailors stumbled into him.

"Watch where you're going," one of the sailors slurred.

"Teach him a lesson, Billy," the other said. Billy wasted no time in lashing out, catching Raymond in the mouth.

It hurt a few seconds later, after sending Raymond sprawling to the cobbles. He scrambled back, trying to avoid the man's iron fist, and was able to scramble out of his grip.

He ran, the two drunks shouting at him for a while until they couldn't keep up. They settled for hurling insults and jeers at him, then turned and sang down the docks away from him.

The side of his head throbbed, and his lip was split and bleeding. Raymond wiped the blood off on his shirt, the rough cloth pulling it away.

In the light of twilight, the docks had lost their romantic air and charm. Now they had turned into something different.

The ships berthed at the piers were monsters, behemoths that lay in wait to devour sailors and goods alike. Who knew what would happen when they went to sea, if they would ever return?

Raymond shivered, the cool air descending and touching his skin, and wished for a rain to wash away the foul-smelling filth on the docks.

He went back to the *Suffolk*, finding it just as he had left, without Isaiah to greet him. He settled into his bunk, and the gentle swaying of the ship rocked him to sleep.

Thumps and cries from the deck above woke him. For a moment he didn't know where he was, and then his senses returned.

Raymond yawned and rubbed the sleep from his eyes. There was no cold water to splash into his face and wake him up, no facilities to relieve himself.

But it was chilly. He shivered in the brisk morning air, which smelled delightfully fresh and salty, and hurried to dress.

The sun was barely up, and the crew was already hard at work loading the ship. Barrels and boxes swung over from the cranes on the dock, lowering their goods to hit the deck and be whisked away into the hold by the crew. The goods went through the first deck by way of an open hatch.

The master was observing the transfer on the quarterdeck, but Raymond didn't feel like talking to him.

The gangplank was busy with traffic, and Raymond had to wait. Eventually, he found an opening and slipped across, joining the throng on the street. He found a place in the alley to relieve himself.

The dagger was a familiar weight now, and comforting. The sun had started to burn off the chill of the night, and he stopped near a bollard to enjoy it.

A ship was sailing into the harbor, most of her sails reefed and a longboat doing a majority of the work by way of towing.

Raymond watched it creep along, curious as to how it would be handled. Crew climbed everywhere around it, like ants, responding to orders and shouts from the first mate.

He rested his arm on the bollard, hard wood worn with age and the harsh sea air, and then leaned against it. He didn't have anything better to do, so he figured this was as good as anything.

The crew moved like monkeys in the rigging, barely hanging on. Their footholds and handholds were sure, confident, and not a man fell in the light breeze.

They towed it closer, with men on the pier waiting and talking among themselves.

Slowly, bit by bit, the ship crept to the dock. When they were close men tossed small ropes across the gap to those waiting on the pier. They quickly made them fast to larger lines, which slipped into the bay and slinked underwater to the ship.

Now, with the rowboat set free, they pulled the behemoth into position until it bumped the pier. Raymond felt the collision, slight from where he was standing, and then the ropes were tied and the gangplank pushed across.

It was done and over with, finished in an hour or two. Raymond yawned and cracked his back, reaching high into the quickly warming sky.

Even with the cool breeze from the sea it would be a warm day. Now he just had to figure out what to do with it.

He didn't want to go too far into town, but staying in the stinking docks didn't appeal to him, no matter how many hiding places there were.

And he couldn't bear to be cooped up in his cabin, not knowing how long he would be on the voyage.

Some exploration was called for. He turned his attention to the dock, searching them for any signs that he was being watched.

Baking bread from somewhere around made his stomach grumble, but he ignored it. Everyone in the street seemed to be in a hurry, rushing from somewhere to somewhere else. A woman stroked a cat in an alley, talking to it. Her hair stood out every which way, and her gaze seemed glazed even from this distance.

Raymond touched the dagger, feeling its coolness against his belly and the hardness of it on his hand. He didn't think anyone noticed but checked to make sure.

The sailors and dockworkers were paying him no notice, other than the annoyed looks if he was in the way. He was too far from the street for the merchants hawking their wares to care about him.

Still, it felt like there were eyes on him. He looked beyond the streets, at the alehouses and shops lining it. They were crooked, jagged things, like the teeth in an old man, mismatched and discolored.

Men were drinking at the bars already, despite the early morning hours, making mirth and joy and not looking at him.

Then, his eyes passed over a shadowed door post, and a hand holding an apple. It went to a man's face, who was watching him, and he took a bite.

Raymond shifted his gaze, trying to act nonchalant. He returned them back after a half a minute or so, discreetly he thought, but the man was still eating, down to the core now.

But he wasn't looking at Raymond. Even after a few minutes, after he wiped his hands on his pants and tossed the apple core into the street, he took no notice of Raymond.

Am I just imagining it? he thought. All at once, the small cabin didn't seem so bad. It was neutral land, a ship at sea, or would be in a few hours.

It would be some protection.

But the man wandered off, walking down the street with no real rhyme or reason, standing out among the hurried and harried masses.

Raymond watched him go, then disappear. He breathed a sigh of relief, but then scolded himself.

"Jumping at shadows. Raymond, shame on you." Still, he left his post and went the other direction, north instead of after the man.

Joining the crowd was like swimming in a fast-moving river. As soon as he stepped inside he was swept along, bumped and prodded by those trying to pass or move around him.

He let it carry him up and away from the docks, hopping out when he could at the next alley.

He had no stomach for the market today and rested in the shade. Some flowers in a pot offered a brief smell of something other than filth, and he took a moment to smell it.

It reminded him of something, but he couldn't put his finger on what.

When he couldn't stand being in the alley any longer Raymond went back into the street, going back the other way.

He slipped into shops, knowing that he wouldn't be buying anything, and perused their wares.

All the time, he kept an eye out for the man he had seen earlier, but he was nowhere to be seen.

Eventually, he couldn't take it any longer and went into an alehouse to eat. It was the cleanest he had seen, just a thin layer of muck on the floor, and it seemed to smell the best.

The barmaid brought him his food, biscuits soaked in fish stew and he ate it. It was too salty, but it satisfied his hunger so he took it without complaining.

"You're a good-looking one," the barmaid said when he had finished, hand resting on his bowl. "What brings you into the gutters with the rest of us?"

Her blouse hung low, and Raymond looked away in embarrassment. He had caught an eyeful. She laughed. "Cat got your tongue?"

"Going on a journey," Raymond said, his voice squeaking. He cleared his throat and tried again. "Going on a journey. I'm leaving tomorrow morning."

"Where to?"

"The east."

"If you're looking for an escape, I might know a thing or two to help." She bit her lower lip and put a hand on his shoulder, slowly caressing his arm.

"Suzy, leave the customers alone," the bartender called.

She wrinkled her eyebrows and put up a pout, then leaned in to whisper in his ear. "I'm off after the evening meal is finished."

Away went his bowl, and Suzy went with it, hips swaying seductively.

Something caught his eye. Raymond turned, but only to see a row of patrons and drunks. One of them had been looking at him, he was sure of it.

He paled, wondering at the sudden interest Suzy had in him. She had been attentive, to be sure, when he had come in. Brought him his food, was polite, but showed no interest otherwise.

So why the sudden change of heart, the invitation?

The warmth went out of the room, and he cast furtive glances around him. The bar was rough, smelled of stale ale and sickness in and around the cooking fish stew. The men were rough looking, their talk as much or more.

Raymond didn't want to be here anymore. He crept to the edge of the bench, then slipped out when he thought no one was watching, not running, but walking at a brisk pace.

As soon as he was out of the door he turned right and walked as fast as he could, glancing back to see if he was being followed.

No one left, as far as he could tell. He stepped out of the crowd and ducked down behind a stack of crates and boxes piled up next to a shop, sitting down to look like he was resting.

Letting his breathing slow, he recovered his heart rate. Was he overreacting? Raymond shook his head, but decided that overreacting was the better option.

He had made too many enemies on this island, and he didn't want to find out what lengths they would go to pay him back.

His appetite was gone, despite the cooking meat that was wafting in from somewhere near. He couldn't stay behind this stack forever, and even though no one glanced his way he thought eventually someone would be by to shoo him off.

The sun was still high in the sky, having passed the zenith, with plenty of time left to kill.

He pushed off the rough ground, rubbed the coarse dirt off his hands and off his pants, and stuck his hands in his pockets.

Whistling, he suppressed his discomfort and walked back to the ship, stopping every so often to take a gander at one of the ships, or examine the wares of a street merchant.

When he wandered up the gangplank, he held his breath until he was on the ship. Crossing that plank made him relieved for some reason. The crew was still hard at work loading, and he took up a position out of the way to watch them work.

Crate and barrel disappeared into the hold, the ship eating them. He wished he could go below, see how they moved and stacked them, but he knew he would just get in the way. This was no time to make the crew or the master angry, so he bore the heat of the day on the deck, checking the docks from time to time for danger.

Isaiah stopped by, wiping the sweat off his brow, as the crew stopped to rest. “Back already? Figured you’d be scarce until the morning.”

Raymond shrugged. “Nothing better to do.”

“Nothing to sample in town? I’d trade positions with you in a heartbeat then,” he said, taking a seat next to the railing and the measly amount of shade it offered.

“How long have you been in port?”

Isaiah squinted and scratched his brown head. “A few days now. Just enough to offload and reload, like Master Goven likes. Always says a ship’s place is at sea, not in port. Besides,” he grinned, “we get into too much trouble in port.”

They talked of the various scrapes Isaiah had been in, including one particularly amusing story involving a fish, a pig, and three barmaids.

Then, all too soon, the mate was rousing the crew to work. Isaiah went back to guiding the cargo down through the hatch, making sure it didn’t hit the sides, and Raymond went back to his observations.

When the man sauntered down the dock, he wasn’t surprised, but he did have a stroke of panic. Raymond slunk down behind the extra sails and peered over it.

The man came with two larger burly men, and he knew they were coming for him. They were stopped at the gangplank by the first mate, and a discussion ensued.

Raymond wished he could hear what they were saying. The man produced a piece of paper to show to the mate, who promptly ignored it and stuck a finger in the man’s chest.

Frowning, they argued back and forth, until Raymond was afraid the man was going to draw weapons with the others and board the ship.

But the sailors had taken notice and were gathered around the mate on the dock or along the edge of the railing of the ship. They too had weapons handy, the hooks of the longshoremen, clubs, and a few cutlasses stowed in handy spots, which made a quick appearance.

The men, deterred by this, made one last entreaty, but after they were spurned turned and left.

The mate scowled and watched him go, then turned back to the crew. "Back to work you lazy dogs," he bellowed. The cutlasses and clubs were put up, and the loading continued.

Raymond watched the first mate march to the master's cabin, wincing when he slammed the door behind him.

A few minutes later, after an agonizing wait, the door opened back up. Raymond considered keeping his hiding place, running back below perhaps, but stood instead and met the master's flashing eyes as he walked to his judgment.

"Mister Ferriss, a word, if you please?" The tone of his voice was firm, and final.

Suddenly dry mouthed, Raymond nodded, and entered the cabin. He had to blink in the lower light for his eyes to adjust, or so he told himself.

The remains of the master's lunch remained on the table, a half a loaf of bread and an empty glass of wine along with the empty plate that once held a side of mutton and vegetables, judging from the remains and the smell.

The master motioned to a chair. Raymond took a seat on the hard surface, unyielding. All the muscles in his body seemed to be tensed up.

The mate stood near the window, scowling at him.

"Is there something you'd like to explain?" The master removed the hurricane cover from the lamp and lit a cigar, puffing it slowly.

Raymond swallowed the lump in his throat. "Some bad men are after me," he said slowly.

The first mate guffawed, and Raymond felt the fear being replaced by the heat of anger.

"Mate Dale tells me three men came to the ship seeking a Mister Raymond Ferriss for thievery and mischief. They had a long list of crimes they accused you of."

"Those are all lies," Raymond said, dropping his gaze.

"Seemed to be a curious long list," the first mate said. He took out a pipe and tapped it against his teeth while Raymond fidgeted beneath the master's stare.

"What answer do you have in respect to these charges?"

"Not guilty, sire. I made the wrong people angry, took what was rightfully mine, and they abused me for it." Raymond met his gaze, trying to feel comfortable and failing. His knees shook like a tree in the wind.

"Dale?" The master returned his attention to the first mate, who was filling his pipe with tobacco. Slow, deliberate movements made him seem like he had not a care in the world.

"Well." The mate took a seat at the table. He closed one eye and looked Raymond over. "The men in question are...known to me."

Raymond reached for it. "You know how they are then, how they're the thieving liars. Willing to take anything a man works for and throw him out on the streets if he asks for it."

"I don't know about that. Is his coin good?" The master nodded. The first mate lit his pipe, puffs of smoke curling around his head as he breathed the fire to life. It filled the cabin with the smell in an instant, thick and dark tobacco. He slightly tilted his head.

"You'll be confined to the ship until tomorrow Mr. Ferriss," the master said, turning to him. "I don't want any sight nor sound of you before we leave."

Raymond blinked. "You're letting me stay?"

The master tilted his head. "Why, Mr. Ferris, you've paid for a seat on this ship, so a seat you will get."

The mate blew a lazy smoke circle in response. "Get below decks now to your cabin."

Relief flooded through him, and Raymond sprung forward, shaking the master's hand vigorously. The man lurched backward in surprise. "Thank you, thank you. You won't regret this."

"I might be already," the master said, prying his hand loose from Raymond's grip. Raymond went to shake the mate's hand, thought better of it from the look he was getting, and rushed to the door. He looked back, the master watching him. "Thank you."

He waved Raymond on, who took his leave.

Giddy, he went down to the cabin he was to share with the two other travelers. He sighed and hopped up into the top bunk, lacing his fingers behind his head. The ship rocked in the tide, the sweet smell of the sea.

"Free at last," he said, tracing the planking of the ship above him. "Free at last."

3

A Parting Gift

"You know I want the information, Betsy. Why can't you give it to me?" Raymond chewed on the end of a cigar, the taste of the fine leaf flooding his tongue.

"Because. That's just something that I can't do. You've known me for enough time to know that." Her mouth drooped in a pout.

"Things can change. Old rules can be...dropped from time to time, certainly?"

"Certainly not. Another?"

"Yes, please." The liquid fire poured into the glass with a satisfying swish. It burned hot despite the chill of the glass. "Fine, as usual."

"I'll put it on your tab." Her voice was deep and husky for a woman, to match her voluptuous body.

"What if I take the information now, and pay you more later for it?"

"Come now, dear. Am I that young and naïve to think a man keeps his word?" Her hand retreated to her chest.

"For a man like me, you would." He grinned at her and tipped his hat. "You'll never find another in the world. You know I'm good for it, all the work we've done together."

"And it's just that. Work. No pleasure in it at all for me."

"Here, let me tell you a story then, about the wild natives that eat men alive and coil their flesh around their heads."

She recoiled. "Too gruesome."

"How about the tale of sunken treasure, guarded by a flock of sharks?"

"Sharks don't travel in flocks, now Mr. Ferriss you must pay for it like all my other clientèle."

"Oh dear, and here I thought I was the only one?" She lit his cigar, leaning in and letting her eyes burn into his. The air tingled, and Raymond started to feel hot under his collar.

"You might be, or you might be one of many." The musician had started another tune, this one dole and sorrowful compared to the light ones he had been playing. "Are you going to ask me to dance?"

Raymond held out his hand. "Would you care to grace me with a dance, milady?"

Her hand fell into his, warm and soft. She moved like a lion, clasping the back of his neck with her other. She pressed tight against him. He didn't mind at all.

"Tell you what. Is there anything else I can do to make up the difference?"

"Yes," she said, then leaned up and whispered in his ear. "Pay the remainder."

"I'm afraid we've been over that." He swung her into an arc, then pulled her back close. "I meant something a little, closer to home, shall we say?"

"What kind of woman do you take me for Raymond?"

Her perfume was heavenly, a mixture of flowers and musk. "My kind, I'm afraid. Out of reach."

She laughed at that, and the song was over. She straightened his collar, patted him on the chest, and looked up into his eyes. "It'll be here for the next few days. Unless someone else takes me up on the offer."

Soft lips touched his cheek. "Goodnight Mr. Ferriss."

"Good night, Betsy." The night had grown late, and Raymond slipped back into his chair, pulling at his shirt.

He could go back to the Groth brothers, get the money from them. Shaking his head, he decided against it. Another pour of the bottle, but then it ran empty. Raymond downed it in one gulp.

It burned all the way down to his stomach, but didn't put out the fire in his heart. She was a desirable woman, but each time he saw her it was harder to bear.

Another man might propose, and he knew that she would refuse him, but he could never stoop to that. It wouldn't be right.

The crowd reveled around him, laughing and talking, drowning out the musician in the corner by the raging fire.

It was too hot for fire, but in a few more hours it would be too cold to sleep. Raymond sighed, picking up the bottle and holding it up to the light. The light danced and flickered along it, distorted by the glass.

There was only one thing to do.

Raymond got up, tipped the bartender, and went to bed.

The next morning came like a hurricane in spring. Rain ran into his room, splashing him awake.

Sputtering, he jumped out of the now soaking bed to shut the window. The wind grabbed it from his hand, forcing against the side of the building with a heavy slam.

He wrestled it back into place, and latched it, giving him some relief from the rain. It still leaked in, dripping into the puddle that had collected on the floor, and slams from around him made him glad he wasn't the only one caught unaware.

The blasted weather couldn't make up its mind. Hot and dry one day, pouring buckets the next. his boots were still dry, luckily, and he slipped them on and dressed in his least wet clothes.

The bottom of his pants were wet, but otherwise he was as dry as he could expect. He spent a few more minutes trying to hang up his bedding to dry and wring out his bedclothes. The washbasin was held up to the window and filled, and then he shaved using its reflection.

The rain lessened when he was done, but he went down for breakfast instead of watching it. There were eggs, fresh from the chickens in back, and some bread. It was a little stale from yesterday, but not bad.

The other patrons were discussing the rain and the bad luck. Who knew what kind of storm this would be, and how many would be caught in it?

The ships were the main concern. Without trade Teruel would be a nowhere, and the fishing fleet kept the larders filled.

When he was done Raymond went out on the porch, stewing as the rain continued its torrent, even harder than before. He wanted that information, needed it.

The problem was getting it. And Betsy kept everything close to the chest. If she had the lead, then it was good. And it would only be for sale for a limited amount of time.

So that left him one choice: get more money.

Easy in principle, hard in execution. The rain drizzled through cracks in the roof in small streams, dripping and dropping in pregnant plops.

A roan animal walked by, pitiful looking, pulling a cart. The man who walked next to it looked just as miserable.

He didn't have enough goodwill in the town to raise money the normal way, so that left him one option.

The rain didn't look like it was going to let up, so Raymond went back to his room for his coat, hiked it up to keep the majority of the rain out, and pushed out into the rain.

It came down like a hammer on him, so thick he almost gasped at the humidity. Adapting to the pressure on his shoulders and head, he worked his way through the sucking, muddy streets.

The shops were open, but the merchants were huddled inside instead of out calling their wares. Raymond kept his head down, hands stuffed in pockets, and kept to his path, although he would rather not do it.

Then, soon enough, he was at the small, ram-shackled hut. Two quick knocks were all it took.

The door cracked, a light shining out into the relative darkness of the storm.

"Who is it?" An eye looked him over, all he could see of the man.

"Raymond Ferriss. I've come to talk to Salty Stu."

The door shut. Raymond checked the street behind him, which was empty of all but the hardiest of travelers.

He waited for what seemed like forever, no porch to protect him from the rain here.

Then, the door opened enough for him to step inside. The doorman slammed it shut behind him with a beefy hand, then stood looming behind him with an outstretched hand.

"Over there."

Raymond followed the pointing finger, stepping onto the creaking ladder that disappeared into the door. He dripped water as he went, some of it falling onto the fireplace stones and sizzling.

He went down, praying that it would hold his weight as it groaned dangerously. The hole smelled of earth and rain, and then he was in a tunnel.

A man waited for him, wiry but dangerous looking and a sword on his hip and daggers tucked in a belt across his chest.

"Morning," Raymond said, flashing a bright smile. The man frowned and knit his eyebrows together, then gestured ahead of him. "Big talker?"

Getting no real response, Raymond followed his lead, going in front of the man down the tunnel. He had a lantern, somewhat blocked by Raymond's body, but it was enough to keep from running into the walls.

When the tunnel split into three roads, the man said his first words. "Left." His voice was husky, and Raymond followed.

Eventually, after a confusing mixture of turns, they came to another ladder and another trapdoor at the top.

This one was solid, and Raymond went up quickly, popping into the back room of what looked like a tavern. There were barrels and boxes, foodstuffs in them and all around.

The only door out of the room was where the man led him, the sounds of conversation behind it.

The door opened into a large room, the centerpiece being the table around which a group of men sat with cards. Smoke hung in the air from pipes and cigars, and men had glasses of spirits in front of them.

"Wants to talk to you," the man said, stepping to the side to let Raymond through.

Raymond took off his hat and bowed. "Good morning, I've heard you're looking for men with... skills. I happened to be in the neighborhood and came by to see what I could offer."

"Offer?" A man threw down a card, scrutinizing him with a cold stare.

A sinking feeling crept into Raymond. He started doubting his decision to come here, but it might be too late for that.

"I can go where your men can't," Raymond said, gripping his hat. "With access comes privilege."

"We've heard of you, Mr. Ferriss." The oldest man at the table drew a deep pull of his pipe, blowing out the smoke. The smell of the strong tobacco reached him across the room. "What use do we have for a treasure hunter?"

Raymond smiled. "All men seek treasure." He shrugged. "I can help find them."

"Treasure isn't found. It's taken." Smoke curled up around his head, wreathing it with a gray haze. "Those who seek it otherwise are fools."

"Then I might be the man to help you take it."

The man gestured. One of the men got up from his seat. Raymond took it, the man standing right behind him, too close.

Raymond wished he would leave him alone, but tried not to let it bother him. For the first time, he wished he had more weapons than the knife hidden in his boot, but then saw the futility of thinking that way.

If it came to that, there would be little he could do. Raymond had walked into the snake's nest. There was only one way out, at least with all his limbs.

"Tell me, do you finish your jobs?" Salty Stu asked. The man to his right shuffled the cards and dealt them.

"Yes. Always."

"Let me tell you about a man who didn't." He pulled out a knife and stuck it into the table. "When we found him, and we did, no matter how far he tried to run, I took a finger for each failed task. And when I ran out of fingers we took the toes. A pity he ran out of those, too."

"I think I see your point," Raymond said, dryly. He picked up his cards. The ship and a sailor, three's each. He played the ship and received a pennant of twos in return.

Not bad, he thought. *If I wanted to win, I think I could.* Brazen Hearts was a common game, and a favorite among the tavern goers.

"Jim, tell him about the job." The eyes bored into his, examining his soul.

The rain let up later that day, the ground soaking up the majority and the rest puddling wherever it could. The sea breeze was fresh, the stench of the town washed away in the storm.

Raymond had a lot of preparation to do. One night, that was all he allotted himself. It would be enough.

Rope, anchors, weapons. It was all there, and the fine clothing he had to pick up to accompany it.

He gathered what information he could, picked up from workers and jilted employees. Builders that hadn't been paid enough to hold their tongue. The work lasted well into the afternoon, but the picture fell together.

It was a beautiful picture, and one that would net him a healthy sum.

If he could pull it off.

A few pieces of gold exchanged in the right hands got him an invitation to the evening meal, and he brushed and prepared until everything was ready.

Examining himself in the dingy mirror, Raymond barely recognized himself. Fluffy shirts, frilly pants, and the stupidest of fashion senses.

"I look like a clownfish, not an angelfish," he muttered to no one in particular. But it was the style, and he only had a few chuckles and jokes as he left.

The trip was quick, from the lower-class area of the city up to the terraces of the rich and famous. His clothes were clean, not a speck of mud on them, which was a feat in and of itself.

He walked up the drive, narrowly avoiding the carriages that would make the task of keeping clothing clean a lot easier.

Music drifted out of the mansion, the evening slipping into twilight. Light blazed from the windows, framed by the golds of the end of the day behind.

The fresh air continued up here, far below the stench of the city and the poor. Gravel crunched under his feet, mixed with seashells, bearing no trace of the storm that passed.

There was a familiar flutter in his gut, and an anticipation of what was to come layered on top.

It was a thrill that started at the bottom of his feet and worked his way up his legs to his heart. It set the great pump working, flushing his body with heat and light.

His eyes narrowed on the door, and the ravishing young woman greeting the entrants with what looked to be her father and mother beside her.

Hair flowed down her head in curls, ringlets that framed her well-proportioned face and blazing blue eyes.

They turned upon him as he walked up. He met them with his most charming smile. She looked away, a flutter of her eyelashes. She tried to regain her conversation, an old man dressed like he was going to a funeral kissing her hand.

"You're too kind," she said.

"I mean every little bit of it, my dear," he said, straightening. "You'll make a jealous husband and I only wish I was younger."

The blush in her cheeks made her face even prettier, and Raymond waited patiently. This would be a good mark.

"Mr. Staunton, we welcome you to our home." The father, stuffy and stern faced, took the old man's hand, shaking it vigorously and ushering him inside. His wife whispered something in his ear and he nodded.

"Good evening, madam." Raymond was next, and took up her hand, kissing her white silk glove. He let his hand linger a heartbeat too long, then released it well within social norms.

It had its desired effect. "Good evening, sir. I believe you have us at a disadvantage." Her voice was light and airy, but she was well spoken.

"Mr. Platton, Jeremy Platton." Raymond bowed again, kissing the mother's hand and then shaking the father's. "I just sailed in on the cutter in the harbor, the *Bounty*, as you can see." They turned to the failing light of the harbor. While they were looking, he winked at the young lady. She never took his eyes off him. "I've come to sample your customs here on Teruel, having come from the Western Seas on a journey of trade and goodwill for my nation, the Trinaisia."

"Oh, how lovely," the mother said. They couldn't see the ship, and he knew it, but there was one out there in case they decided to go looking in the night.

"If I could get your opinion of the shipping routes in the area, I'd be much obliged." Raymond stepped up to the man. He felt the woman looking at him, but ignored it. They engaged in a brief conversation, just enough to establish some bona fides, and Raymond slipped inside.

The house smelled of flowers and opened up into an inner courtyard where guests mixed and mingled. A group of musicians played on instruments he had never seen before, the source of the music. Too refined and stuffy for Raymond's taste, he moved to the tables spread along one side of the courtyard.

This was where the display of wealth was, and judging from the smell of it, was where he was going to find himself most of the night.

It started with breads, pastries, and sweets arranged between sweet-smelling flowers and roses. It continued with strange meats, both hot and cold, and dishes of varying sorts, all of which seemed to be expensive.

Capping off all of it was a large bowl of punch on a huge silver platter. Raymond swallowed at the sight of it, if it were real silver it would have fetched enough to feed ten families for ten years.

He had no doubt it was real.

There were small porcelain plates for the guest to use and Raymond quickly filled his up, mouthwatering.

He had to take a cup of the punch, but decided to eat first. Being discreet, and tucking in behind a column, Raymond took his first bite of a pastry.

It crumbled in his mouth, flaking and crispy. Inside was a surprise of creamy, fruity delight. It lasted another two bites and was gone.

The rest of it was just as good, if not better, and the meats smelled wonderfully spicy. He went back another time, careful to make sure there were different groups around, and then took a cup of the punch as well.

It was fruity and rounded out with mulled spices, fresh on his palate for the warm summer evening. These people knew how to throw a party.

When he was finished, and eying a third trip, Raymond settled down away from everyone else to observe.

There were dancers now in the center of the courtyard, their feet clicking on the paved patio in time to the beat. It was an ornate dance, full of twisting and turnings, bowing and curtsying, and all manner of strange act, and seemed to go on forever.

Raymond was just thinking he'd got the hang of it when he felt a hand on his elbow.

"Mr. Jeremy, you seem to have hidden yourself quite well." It was the young woman, eyes bright and smiling, a flush upon her cheeks.

"Oh, I'm no dancer Miss Halloway. Just trying to keep out of the way."

"Surely you have dancing in your country?" She took her spot at his side, observing them with him. He wouldn't be surprised if she was gone in a few minutes, whisked away by some young suitor.

"I'm afraid it would seem simple compared to your..." he waved a hand toward the dancing, "elegant movement."

"With the right partner, our elaborate dancing would seem simple as well."

"I see. Unfortunately, I came alone."

"There are many young, eligible bachelorettes here. I'm sure you'll find one, eventually." She waved to someone in the crowd. "Excuse me, sir." With another lingering touch, she was gone, wading into the crowd to join a group of friends.

Raymond's eyebrows shot up. It wasn't what he was expecting, but she could play a good game of it. The right touch, but enough of a chase to goad pursuit.

Tonight would be fun.

All his information indicated she was single, but as the night wore on, he wasn't so sure. She was surrounded by suitors, danced with men of all stripes, and laughed with her female friends in between.

Raymond made his move at the end of a particularly quick movement, while everyone was still flushed and out of breath.

"Miss Halloway, I've observed you are a good dance partner and a gentle hand." he extended his own. "Would you grace a poor foreigner the chance to learn a new custom?"

She patted her neck, glistening with sweat. At first he thought she was going to refuse, a glimmer of something in her eye. Was it predatory or confusion?

Either way, she placed her graceful hand in his. "Certainly, Mr. Platton."

Raymond moved in as the musicians started the next piece. He put one hand on the small of her back and shifted the other to cup hers. It was a slow piece, and Raymond let her lead the first few measures, struggling to keep up with the steps and observe the others to get the hang of it.

"Mr. Platton, I do believe we'll make a civilized man out of you," Miss Halloway said. Her eyes were glowing, her lips soft. She moved her hand, soft but firm, on his back. With it she guided him, pressing him left or right to move his feet in the right direction.

"With you as a dancing partner, I believe I can do anything." His blood was flowing now, heart pumping in time to the music. She was breathing faster, sharp, quick breaths that betrayed her calm demeanor. He sensed her blood was up, too.

"How long will you be in Teruel?"

"Long enough. I long to be back home, and the sea calls me from time to time." He looked at her. "There are treasures out there, Miss Halloway. Wonderful treasures just waiting for a man to find."

She laughed, a wonderful bright sound. "You're a treasure hunter?"

"Of a kind."

"And what kind of treasure do you seek the most?"

"The rare and beautiful. The kind I can hold in my hand." He squeezed her tighter, feeling her against his body, and spun her around in a twirl. It was a strange move, one he had learned long ago on a distant island none of these party-goers had ever heard of.

It attracted attention, and Miss Halloway's eye opened wide, her lips parting.

"Did you like that, Miss Halloway?"

"Please call me Julie." They were back to the normal steps. "And yes, I did."

"There are places out there you've never dreamed of. Grand places, wonderful places. Dangerous places."

"And they're filled with dangerous men?"

It was his turn to laugh. "Of a kind. Some of them venture out and prowl the peaceful waters, looking for young women to devour."

"Then I must have a protector."

"Lucky for you," Raymond said, flashing a smile that made her eyes flutter, "I also protect things. Treasures included."

"Hmm." Her eyebrows raised. "Do you indeed?"

"It's getting stuffy." The song was coming to a close, and Raymond dipped her sensuously enough to be scandalous, in the wrong circles. "How about we go somewhere else? The gardens, perhaps?"

"Why, Mr. Platton, whatever do you mean by it?"

"Please call me Jeremy." The last note played, and then the hall erupted in applause. "I'm sorry, I'm new here and lost. I need a guide."

She gave him a questioning look, then glanced around. "Come on." She took his hand and pulled him through the crowd, which was pressed into the room like sardines packed into a barrel.

Then, they were free of the smell of sweat and heat of the bodies and out into the cool, sweet air of the night. They laughed and turned to each other.

"Come this way, into the garden, Jeremy." She looked up from under her eyelashes, and the look set his heart thumping.

But he had a job to do. This was just a mark, one that would be gone in the morning. He couldn't do anything with this girl of lasting significance. He would be found out in a heartbeat.

But she looked gorgeous in the moonlight as it reflected off her hair, her smile a delight in the flower laced scent of the sea breeze. There wasn't enough chill in the night to take away the heat of this moment.

He followed under a trellis, and she slipped her hand into his arm, hugging tight to his.

"Careful now, Julie. You might catch a chill out here in the city air."

Her body was warm, and she pressed it tighter against his. He could feel everything, from the straps of her dress to her soft, supple skin through the cloth. "I think I can find the heat to keep me warm."

They walked through the garden, chatting and flirting. He was at his most charming, regaling her with tales of the sea.

"You love it, don't you?" There was a hint of sadness in her voice.

"The sea is a fickle mistress. At one point she's calm, blowing from the right quarter to rush you on through the spray of saltwater and the call of the birds. The next moment is waves and lightning, threatening to pull you deep into the dark that never ends." He shook his head. "I don't know what kind of man would love that."

"Then it's the adventure that you love. The way the sea opens up to you, allows you to find what others have not." He turned, her eyes sparkling.

He couldn't do this. He had a job to do and wouldn't survive more than a few nights if he didn't. And he had to think about the information at the end of it, the price that he was willing and able to pay.

"I feel she calls me. There's no way I can be wedded to the land." The words came out, tasting like ash in his mouth.

The bitterness was needed, and Julie turned away. "Is there anything that could take you away from it?"

"Nothing, I'm afraid." Her arm went stiff on Raymond's, then she pulled it free.

"I see. Well, I'll leave you to it, Mr. Platton."

He thought she might react like this, wanted desperately to reach back to her, take her in his arms and beg forgiveness. Promise her the world. What was he thinking, he barely knew her?

Instead, he stiffened, gave a brief bow, and said good night. She walked off, slightly faster than what would seem an easy stride, back to the house.

He watched her go, mournful of what could have been but focused on the priority of the night. He had his access, now it was time to put it to good use while everyone was distracted.

The window glittered in the moonlight, reflecting the stars in the sky. It was well into the early morning hours of the next day by now, but the party showed no signs of stopping.

All the better for him. He took off his jacket, unloosening the rope tied carefully around his midsection, and tied it to the grapple he had shoved down his boot.

Taking a deep breath, and hoping the musicians would be playing for the next few seconds, Raymond swung the grapple in a circle, then loosed it at the height of its arc.

It sailed into the air, alighting on the edge of the windowsill with a clatter, then looping around it a few times.

He gave it a good yank, seating it, and tested his weight on it.

It held. He gave one last look into the ballroom and courtyard, to the dancing figures and well-dressed men and women inside.

That wasn't his world. This was his world, a world of searching and finding, of doing the hard jobs when they needed to be done.

He couldn't spend his life attached to a woman far above his station in life. The wealth, the boringness, the stuffiness of afternoon tea and parties that would make him want to tear his hair out. He wouldn't give up his life for the world of it.

And, he suspected, she wouldn't give up her world for his. Never having a place to call home, always on the move, going from place to place in search of the next great treasure.

No, it was good they were parting. But, as he climbed that rope, a bit of his heart pained and shriveled in sadness.

The smell of the roses in the garden greeted him when he finally got to the balcony, breathing and stiff.

He wrestled an arm over the edge of the railing and pulled himself onto the hard marble floor with an impact. He stopped, waiting to hear if he had been found.

There was nothing but the sounds of music and laughter drifting up from below. Guards patrolled outside the walls, but they were concentrated at the entrance of the house to keep the party-goers safe. One of the blind spots of being so secure, you never expected those thieves to get in another way.

The door inside was locked, but a quick pick from the thin lock-pick he brought with him sorted it out, opening with a soft click.

He was inside a second later, shutting the door behind him. It was the library, as he had been told. He sighed in relief and crept cautiously across the room to the safe beneath the desk.

It was locked, unfortunately. However, he had prepared for this. Now he took out a finer lock picking set, designed specifically for this task.

The lock was thick, but the mechanism inside was made by a master. There would be bolts that held the door shut on all four sides. Forcing it open was a fool's errand, taking it with him impossible due to its weight.

That left him no option but to try and open it by coercion and cunning. The pick resisted slipping into the lock, until he found the right angle, but eventually it did go. Some exploration found a set of pins that needed to be raised, but there would be a catch.

These pins would have a false set, and if he tried it there, the safe would remain forever locked until it was broken apart.

Raymond closed his eyes, focusing all his effort into feeling the pick and holding tension on the lock with a tensioner.

There were six pins. He started at the front, pushing it up until the tensioner set it in place, then he let up ever so slightly to see if it was still there.

It was.

He moved on, repeating the process with each pin. A few didn't stay, a false set, and had to be pushed up even farther, one too far.

Sweat was now collecting on his forehead, the pressure feeling like a weight on his shoulders.

He thought he heard footsteps in the hallway and stopped, eyes flying open to look to the door.

His head was just above the top of the desk, giving him enough view to see the light from the bottom of the door.

There were footsteps, and they were coming this way, clicking on the marble with a steady rhythm that could only mean one thing.

A patrol.

Raymond breathed out, holding his instruments in place and hoping that the man would keep walking.

There was no such luck. The footsteps came to the door, obscuring the light beneath it, and stopped.

Go on, go to another door. There was a rasp of metal from the door. Something turned in the lock, a key, then clicked it open.

Raymond ducked down, heart pounding. His hand was starting to ache from holding the right tension in the lock, but he couldn't let go now.

Back against the desk, he saw his rope still attached to the balcony railing, as plain as day.

And then the door opened, admitting in a stream of light.

His body went cold, and his breath caught in his throat. Heart pounding, he waited at the desk as the light lessened, obscured by the shadow of the man.

It paused there for a moment, what felt like forever, eyes searching the room for anything out of place.

Raymond's eyes fixed on the rope, still attached, hanging limply in the calm night. One little puff of sea breeze so common and everything would be over. He couldn't fight them all and take what he came for.

So, he waited.

Second by agonizing second, time slipped away until it was almost gone. He was sure he would be caught, and when the man left and the door shut, he couldn't believe it. The night remained calm.

But it was true. The key turned in the lock, the footsteps went back down the passageway, and he was alone once again.

He had to regain his breath and slow his heart from impossibly fast to excited. The smell of the library filled his lungs, leather and paper mixed with stale smoke, and he eased some of the tension off the lock to give his hand a rest.

A few more moments and he thought he was finished, the last pin sliding into what felt like a certain set.

He breathed out, then pushed the tensioner, closing one eye.

It felt resistance, then sprang forward as the lock shifted.

It was open.

He swung the lock the rest of the way, retracting the locking bolts with a scrape, and opened it up.

Raymond shuffled through the papers, taking a few that looked like they could be exchanged safely, and then took what he was looking for and wrapped it up in cloth and tucked it into his shirt pocket.

Something caught his eye in the moonlight, a stack of papers tied with a bow or string. He couldn't tell which.

A strange scent came from them, and he held the stack close to his nose. Perfume.

A ladies perfume.

Something told him it wouldn't be the mistress of the house's.

For a second, he almost took it, thinking of the value it could bring, but then he put it back.

He didn't have the heart to do it. Not to her. Tearing up her family like that.

He shut the safe door, spinning the lock until it sprung shut with a clank and every bolt was back in place.

Now was the hard part. He tried to erase any trace of his existence, then went back to the balcony.

Somehow, he had to get down and bring the rope with him.

Luckily, he knew how. He untied the grapple and unwrapped the rope from the balcony. A few particular wraps in the moonlight and a new knot was now tucked into place.

After swinging one leg over the railing, then the other, he tested his work with all of his weight.

It held.

Below him, the gardens were quiet, no guards in sight.

He went down, checking for movement in the garden. A young couple were tangled up in the corner, thinking they were alone and wrapped in each other's embrace.

Raymond left them alone, feet hitting the gravel below with a crunch. He let go of the rope, releasing the tension, then gave a quick, sharp yang on the rough rope.

Down it came, in a bundle, and he wrapped it around his midsection again. He retrieved his coat, dressed himself, and brushed himself into service.

The party was still in full swing as he went in. He thought about staying all night, then decided against it. It would be less suspicious, but then again, he had just had a fight with the lady of the house as far as anyone knew, and thus had a perfect chance to compose himself in the gardens with the fresh air and storm out.

He opted to fill a plate, as long as they were offering, and ate it. She wasn't to be found.

Raymond wandered a bit longer, uncomfortable at the staring and the attention. Whispers seemed to follow him, and he tried to dismiss them because of his imagination.

He was starting to get uncomfortable. Even though he wanted one last look at her, he knew it wasn't worth it. He left the party, sparing one last glance back at the house.

Something fluttered in one of the windows. A drape, perhaps, moved by a draft.

He thought he would be satisfied, the work pulled off without a hitch, but there was a strange sensation of incompleteness.

Wandering through the streets of Teruel, he took his time to get back.

There would be enough money for the information now, if Salty Stu was to be trusted, and one more adventure to be had. The sea was calling him, and all the things it contained. Some right where he could reach them, others too deep for even the hardiest of submarines.

He stopped by a house overlooking the sea, leaning on the rough door post and fingering the small package that would give him what he wanted.

Moonlight scattered off the ocean, like bits of glass shimmering on blackest of inks. The ships rocked in the harbor.

One would be taking him to where he wanted to go.

He looked back as he left, up to the terraces of the rich. A treasure hunter was what he was, what he had always been. There was no room in his heart for another love.

He whistled a tune, soft and mournful, as he walked back to his own world.

4

Misgivings Among the Night

Ale sloshed as the mug slammed into the table, and Raymond took a seat in the empty chair.

He wobbled in it, then leaned forward. "I don't like that look, Harold."

The men at the table looked at each other over their cards. The man in question, large, rotund, but hiding something dangerous beneath those layers of fat, narrowed his eyes. "Excuse me?"

Raymond stood up, knocking the chair backwards, and pushed his finger into the hair-covered chest. "There is no excuse for you, you big, fat blubbering whale."

Gasps from the women nearest. Men backed up.

"Take it back," Harold said, his jowls jiggling in rage. His eyes were mere slits now, and one hand was at his side.

"I'll take nothing— "

"Raymond, why don't you come back to our table?" A man gently removed Raymond's finger from Harold's chest, then wrapped an arm around him. "He's very sorry, Harold." He lowered his voice to a whisper. "And very drunk. He's had a hard day."

"He's about to have a hard fist in his face if he talks about me like that."

"Why don't you get back to your game with a round on Raymond?" The man gave him a winning smile. The mention of free booze turned away the anger bubbling at the table. Monk tipped his hat and waved to the bartender. In a few seconds, over the protests of Raymond, he led the man away, struggling to keep him on his feet, to a table secluded in the corner.

Raymond glared at him. "You should have stayed out of it."

"If I had, you'd be flat on the floor," Monk said. Raymond reeked of alcohol. "How long have you been here?"

Raymond picked up a mug and raised it to his lips. Monk took it away.

"Something wrong?" he asked, taking a sip from his own ale. Raymond hiccupped. "Wrong, wrong? How about the end of the world?" He slurred his words, hanging onto the end syllable just a second too long. "The end of days. The judgment. Death and mayhem."

"Funny," Monk said dryly. "I missed the seas boiling on my way over."

Raymond buried his head in his hands. The fire crackled happily in the soot-stained fireplace. Years of candle wax dripped down the mantel. He moaned.

"Why? Why is this happening to me?"

Monk took another sip. Warm, but the taste wasn't bad. Plenty of hops. "What's happening?"

"I'm getting married," Raymond moaned.

Monk's eyebrows shot up. "Raymond Ferris, married?" The thought of it made him chuckle, then guffaw.

Raymond buried his head on the table.

Monk's laughter faded, then his smile too. "You're serious."

All that came from Raymond was another low moan, like a dog that had just been kicked.

“Well, who’s the lucky lady? I’m surprised someone was able to tie down the great lady killer Raymond Ferris.”

“You don’t want to know.”

“Ah,” Monk said, a twinkle in his eye. He pulled his chair closer to Raymond and put an arm round his shoulder. “So, I do know her.”

Raymond turned his head the other direction. Monk signaled to the bartender, and a few seconds later the serving girl presented him with another mug.

Monk held it near Raymond, then wafted the top in his direction.

He couldn’t escape the smell, and soon a hand reached out and took it. Lips followed suit, great gulps of it nearly emptying it halfway.

“Why does she look at me that way?” Raymond asked, wailing in frustration. “The way her eyes are so warm and inviting. The look she gives stops my heart cold.”

“I’m surprised it wasn’t frozen already.”

“It should have been.” Raymond tried to slam his fist on the table, but missed and caught the edge, nearly falling over.

Monk caught him and steadied him.

Two tables over, a group of men erupted in laughter. Monk stole a glance. They were preoccupied with something else.

“My life is over. No more adventures. No more treasure hunting. No more thrill of almost having your heart cut out by pygmy natives four feet tall covered in tattoos.” Raymond took another drink.

“Are you sure that’s going to happen?”

“I’m sure of it.” Raymond sighed and leaned his head on his hand, the elbow on the table. “I’ll be a family man before long. Bundles of babies, little ones running along trailing snot.”

“I see you’ve thought about this quite a bit. Have you ever considered not getting married, if you’re so sure it isn’t what you want?”

“But that’s the thing. I’m not sure it *isn’t* what I want.“ Now he pulled at his hair, setting down an empty mug. “Oh, the pain that pulls at my heart. Fun and adventure on one side and,” Raymond looked at Monk, a sly, drunk smile on his lips. “You know, the other thing, on the other hand.”

“Ah, the tender embraces of the fairer sex. Can’t say I’m tempted, to tell you the truth.” Monk looked off in the distance. “But the sea is my love and holds my heart. Much like adventure and thrill seem to hold yours.”

Raymond nodded solemnly. “That’s why I’m torn. A battle between loves. I’ve never thought about it that way. Did I ever tell you how we met?”

“Who?”

“Julie.”

“Julie? As in Julie Halloway?” Monk gave him an appraising look. “You do like to play with fire, don’t you?”

“The very one. Almost took off my finger she did.” A misty look came over Raymond. “And a knife at my throat, all for paying her the mildest of compliments.”

“Sounds...enchanting.” Raymond had always been something of a mystery to Monk. Rarely in town, and always after some ancient treasure or another. He was likable enough, but Monk didn’t trust him as far as he could tie him.

“They say whales mate for life, up far to the north,” Monk said. Raymond held his empty mug in the air, waving it at the bartender. The bartender narrowed his eyes, but poured another one. “But it takes a pack of females to do it.”

“Whales? Never liked ’em.”

“Do you want to hear how?”

“Are you going to tell me even if I say no?”

Monk smiled. "They chase down the male, four of five of the females, after luring him in with their song. Then they attack."

"They're vicious, charging in and using their blunt, large noses to wound. The males try to fight back, but it's no use. The females overwhelm him with numbers."

"Sounds like my kind of night." A pretty little barmaid handed him a mug, and Raymond looked her over with an appreciative eye.

While he was doing that Monk took a pipe from his jacket and lit it using the candle from the table. Puffs of sweet-smelling tobacco rose from the bowl. "They wear the male down over hours, keeping it from swimming away. Then, when the male has lost all will to fight and run," Monk spread his arms. "They present his mate, ready and willing. He can't resist, and once the deed is done—"

"It's the end of his life forever."

"I was going to say he never chooses another one, but that works too. You could say that."

"Have you ever bought a woman pearls?" Raymond asked.

"I think you missed the point..."

"I saw your point." Raymond raised an eyebrow and puffed out his cheeks. "You haven't answered the question."

"No."

"Well, I have." He sounded ashamed and hung his head. "And flowers. Flowers, confound it!"

"Perhaps being married won't be so bad as you think. Some men take to it rather well I hear." Monk wasn't going to say anything about Julie Halloway. He wasn't sure Raymond would survive, let alone thrive, with her.

"And some men think they can lead a donkey to water just because they can ride a broken nag."

Puffing on his pipe, letting loose curls of smoke wrap around his head, Monk sat back and examined his drinking companion.

The working girls giggled, slapping hands playfully that found their way into sensitive areas.

The Flying Fish Inn wasn't his regular, but he had a hankering for some mutton. He never expected to be sitting here having this conversation. "Have you thought about not getting married at all?"

"Haven't you asked that already?"

"It seems to bear repeating," Monk said dryly.

"I've gone and done something stupid. I've given her the ring of Calasia."

"What's that?"

"You can't tell me you haven't heard of the ring of Calasia?" Raymond's mouth hung open.

A few moments of receiving Monk's blank stare back at him shut his mouth. "Well, I thought it was a rather common thing to know."

"In who's circles?"

"True, you're simply a sailor and a — " Raymond cut off, looking at him with a rather peculiar look. "Let me buy you a drink. I owe you for what you did to get me out of that scrape I was going to put myself in."

"I thought you wanted to get into a fight?" Monk asked, while Raymond signaled for more ale.

"To feel a man's fist in your gut, his knuckles on your cheek." Raymond sighed. "It's been months since I've had a good tavern brawl, even longer since I've been in a duel of any real consequence."

Monk took up the frothy mug that the pretty little barmaid brought. She was young, and lithe, and looked over her shoulder at them. He looked back to Raymond, thinking about the girl, and tipped the mug in his direction before taking a drink.

All of a sudden Raymond perked up. The fire cracked particularly loud, and a puff of white smoke entered the air from the fireplace. Monk's pipe mingled with the smoke, combining the smell of pipe tobacco and oak.

"I've got an idea." Raymond was eying him slyly.

"You'll go to Julie, tell her everything was a mistake and call it all off?" he offered.

"What!" Raymond drew back comically, as if struck. "No, I value my life, but you have a ship and I have feet that can take me on that ship."

"Oh no. You're out of your mind."

"By Jove, a ship got me into this mess, and a ship can take me out." Raymond was smiling ear to ear now, whether by the idea or ale induced Monk couldn't tell.

"Absolutely not. I don't have room even if I wanted to."

"You can't leave me here to die."

"Marriage isn't death."

"Then why haven't you done it?"

"I told you, no one would have me. My first and true love is the sea."

"Bah, what a fickle mistress that is." Raymond slumped back into his chair, completely deflated like an empty sack of potatoes. "Then what do you counsel, Monk? Throw myself into the sea?"

"What do you think of Julie?" He puffed again on his pipe, blowing a ring of smoke with a well-placed mouth.

"I-I love her. I can't get away from here, even when I sleep, I dream about her. Those hips, that hair, the eyes!" Raymond clutched at his face, pulling at his beard.

"Well, sir, it seems to me that I have only one thing to counsel." He took a sip. Raymond stared at him, waiting.

Finally, he could take it no more. "Go on then, out with it."

"I advise you to get a good night's rest, put on your boots, and marry this woman."

"I was afraid you were going to say that." Raymond pulled at his ale, nearly draining it in one go. He hiccupped. "And I can't see any other way out of it."

When Monk looked closely, he thought he saw Raymond's eyes drifting in different directions. *How much had he had to drink?*

"From what I hear, there is a way out of it, or so my mate says."

"What's that?" Raymond asked.

"Death." Monk raised his mug to his lips. Raymond chuckled at that.

"I'm afraid that's the way I'd go if I left her now. Not that I want to." Raymond looked out the window into the night sky. It was too bright in the room to see any stars, but they were out there scattered like sand.

Men had left over the last few minutes they were talking, the night dying out as they wandered back to their homes or their ships. Now the room was half empty, and half again as stuffy with the cool breeze from the sea flowing through the open window.

It brought with it the smell of the sea. Fresh, salty, with a scent unlike any other. Monk loved it, and it felt like home.

"Will you still seek your treasures, then go on your adventures?"

Raymond sat for a while, swaying in his chair. Monk was just about to repeat himself, thinking that he hadn't heard him, when Raymond spoke.

"I don't know how. It's in my blood, goes down to the root of my soul. Julie has said she'd permit it, from time to time, but expects me to be a more respectable gentleman. I can't give it up." His eyes glistened, from sadness or happiness, Monk couldn't tell which.

For a time, they sat in silence, but then Monk realized that Raymond was lost in thought. "Well, Mr. Ferriss. I must excuse myself." He put out the remains of his pipe, tapping out the ashes, and finished his ale. From his pocket he produced two coins, which he gave to the pretty barmaid to take to the bar.

"We've known each other a good while now, haven't we, Monk?"

"I should think tis been a few years."

Raymond turned to him, took up his hands in his and looked deep into his eyes. "Remember me Monk, if I come around. Remember the other side of me, the wild side untamed. And never find yourself a woman."

Astonished, Monk nodded, then couldn't find the words to say anything else. He pulled his hands free, bid Raymond a good night, then left him slumped in his chair at the corner of the tavern.

He looked back as he stepped into the night, wrapping his cloak tighter around him in the chill. Raymond was visible in the window, the flickering of the fire.

Monk gazed in wonder, swore off any semblance of marriage for himself, and slipped his pipe back into his pocket.

He left Raymond in the tavern, contemplative about his life and future, and returned to his life on the sea.

5

Ring of Calasia

Something slithered in the dark, then touched his outstretched arm. Raymond froze as his heart beat faster.

His chest was pressed up against the cool wall, sapping the heat even through his clothing, with his hand and shoulder extended inside.

It was supposed to be here. Why couldn't he feel it?

The slithering thing hissed, then a scaly body wrapped around his hand and went up his arm.

Raymond closed his eyes and breathed. The moist air of the damp cave was soggy and metallic, with an overriding smell of must layered on top.

His new friend stopped, then curled up on his warm hand. The weight was almost more than he could bear, even holding onto the rocks with his hand.

Well, I'm in the pickling jar now. For not the first time this day he cursed his bad luck, then asked himself why he was doing this.

A pretty face warmed his heart and steadied his hand. Was that the flick of a tongue on his ear?

"Well now, old fellow," Raymond said, his voice echoing in the dark. "We can't have you sit there all day."

Slowly, very slowly, he brought his other arm around. It wouldn't fit past his chest. The movement disturbed the snake, that's what it had to be, and he held his breath.

It slithered up his shoulder now, and onto his head. Raymond swallowed, hoping it wouldn't find his neck.

It didn't, and continued onto his other arm, giving him enough strength to let go of the wall and step back.

He bent his knees until his fingers found dirt with rock underneath. Raymond tipped to the left, urging his new friend into a more appropriate location.

It went, coaxed by the flicker of his torch stuck in the sand. Black scales reflected the light, shifting and scraping like so many plates of mail.

Raymond, after a quick breath and recovery, returned to the crack, feeling around.

Rock. more rock. Rock again.

Oh, what's that? Rock.

He shifted deeper, well aware that he wouldn't fit much more, but he had to have this.

It was going to be a present.

His hand fumbled, disturbed some sort of creepy crawly that skittered across his hand, tickling his skin.

Raymond frowned and jammed himself as far as he could go.

Rock, then...something else.

He smiled, then closed his hand around the metal lever and gave a sharp pull.

Something clicked, and across the way the rock swung open.

That was it.

Raymond let go and pulled out his arm.

Or tried to. His hand wouldn't move, his chest pinned between two sections of rock wall.

Points of rock were digging into his skin, ones he had ignored trying to get to the lever.

Now, they were burning. Raymond squirmed and shifted, but despite his movements, was stuck fast.

And it looked like his fuss had woken his new friend. A head peered his way, testing the air with a forked tongue.

He had to get out before things turned...interesting.

Stay calm. There has to be a way out of this.

His pack was out of reach, next to his torch. The crevice, if he remembered right, was tighter at the top than the bottom.

He tried going down. It didn't work.

The snake was on the move now. Raymond wasn't sure this time it was looking for a warm place to sleep. Beady black eyes stared at him, the heat pointed directly in his direction.

In a great s, it started to come close.

Raymond breathed out and pulled. He thought he felt himself move.

With a great breath, he expelled everything in his lungs until they hurt, then dropped down.

His clothes tore, and skin went with it, but he tumbled out of the crack onto the floor.

The snake was feet away. Raymond saw it and knew it was going to attack.

He went for his knife.

It sprung.

The blade caught its head in midair, long, pointy fangs dripping venom parted from a body.

Raymond struggled to his feet as the head snapped at the air, unaware that it wasn't attached. The body spasmed wildly, and he backed up.

The throes calmed, then stopped.

The snake was dead. Raymond breathed a sigh of relief. He went over to the torch and examined his shoulder.

It was cut in a few places, but didn't look all that bad. He took out a wad of bandages and wrapped it.

It wasn't pretty, but it would do. He would need to get something on it as soon as he was out of here.

His eyes returned to the small cubby, open and itching to be relieved of the contents.

The torch sputtered as he picked it up, protesting its movements and spitting off black, foul-smelling smoke.

Raymond licked his lips. Salty, from the air, with a hint of rock. He spat and checked for traps.

It didn't look like there were any, but he took his time. Nothing above that would drop on him, no small holes in the rock on either side.

As a precaution he kicked at the sand beneath, uncovering it until he got to rock. It was solid when he tapped on it, a healthy noise.

He hoped they were still there when he got back, not that he knew how long he had been down here at this point. Time seemed to stretch on in the caves, with no sun to guide him.

He was avoiding looking in, and he knew it.

What would this do to them? Am I even ready?

He paced back and forth, chewing on a knuckle. *Would she even like it?*

Finally, he could take it no longer, and shoved the torch above, looking in.

The red glitter was the first thing he saw, the ruby so deep in color it seemed to pale the gold pedestal it was on in comparison.

Round, polished, it was just the right size for a lady's ring, although it would be awkward for a hand her size to carry.

It sat there lifeless, but a thing desired and wanting to be desired.

Raymond stood back, resting his hand on his chin. He knew at once he was going to get it, there was no question about that.

The question was, what dirty little trap had they lain on it?

He squinted, examined, looked. Every crack was scrutinized, every discontinuity a clue.

The golden pillar was continuous and looked solid. He wanted to touch it, to see if it was pure gold, but held himself back from its dull shine.

The cubby was carved in the rock, the door open. It looked like it was on a hinge, a single piece of stone on the left side. It was back on the inside, and he was sure it would be impossible to tell it from the surrounding rock if shut.

He was delaying, and he knew it.

"Come off it." Raymond turned. Somewhere down deeper in the cave a drip of water plunked loud enough to be heard over the flickering hiss of his torch.

It would go out eventually. He couldn't stay down here forever.

He shoved a hand in his pack, rummaging around all the supplies until he found it. He pulled the leather pouch out, slick with oil to keep out the water, and judged the size. It was big enough.

Gingerly, Raymond reached forward. Just as he was about to cross the plane of the opening, he stopped.

He took out his axe, flipped the handle around and poked it inside.

Faster than he could blink, a blade sliced down into the shaft, jerking it out of his hand and cutting halfway through before it jammed.

Everything on his body puckered. "Glad that wasn't my finger," he muttered.

When his heart rate came down from the instant jump, he tried the handle of his knife next.

Nothing. Apparently, the trap was spent.

Raymond chuckled as he thought about it. "Leave with a gift, eh? I've got two hands like everyone else."

He reached in, confident he was safe, but not fully. His finger touched the ruby.

It was cool, and smooth like glass. His hand trembled as it closed around the ring.

A thrill went through his body. He held his breath, then took it.

The base shone, reflecting the light of the torch, but now it was empty.

Raymond froze, listening. All he could hear was the flicker of the torch. He slipped the ring inside, fully intending to turn and go back.

But the base was gold. He hesitated, almost turning. He reached back in and pressed a fingernail against the top.

It sank in. Not much, but enough.

Giddiness ran through him. It was a nice little prize, if it turned out to be solid.

And, he realized, might offset the cost of the ship and its crew.

A sloppy grin grew on his face, and he curled his toes in delight.

This trip was turning out alright after all.

He scooped it up in one go, delighting at its heft and weight. Into the leather pouch it went, joining the ring.

Raymond slung his pack on his back, picked up the torch, and walked back through the cave to the entrance.

As he did, he whistled a happy little tune. He stretched his arms. His limbs were tired, but not that bad.

Something caught his attention as he worked around the stalagmites and over rocks. He stopped whistling and cocked his head to the left to hear better.

It sounded like scraping.

Like rock on rock.

Like a door closing.

Raymond's eyes widened, and he broke into a run. *Stupid. Couldn't let it go.*

Light played over the walls, his torch in threat of being snuffed out from his speed. His feet found solid rock most of the time, but every few steps he stumbled, only to pick himself up again and keep going.

It felt warm in here now, and sweat was tricking down his brow. Heart racing, breathing fast, Raymond turned the corner and saw the door at the end of the cave.

It was over halfway down by now. He sprinted the rest of the way.

He threw the pack in first, ripping it off his back and dropping the torch. There wasn't much room left for him.

Raymond dropped to the dust, sending a spray of it in his face, and crawled forward. His knees scraped on the rock, and the rough, rock bottom of the door pressed against this back.

Sucking in his stomach, Raymond grabbed the ground and pulled as hard as he could.

He was through. The door slammed shut as he pulled his legs through, engulfing him in complete and utter darkness.

He lay there, panting, heart pounding in his chest.

He blinked, but it made no difference in the pitch black. The chill of the cave cooled his body.

Raymond groped around, trying to find his pack. *Had to drop the torch.*

Maybe it wasn't the best trip, after all.

It wasn't in the circle of his hands, so he got to his knees and shuffled in the direction he thought was forward.

There was a wall to his left after a few feet, and then his creeping hands felt a strap, then pulled the pack out of the blackness.

He wasn't a fan of the dark. Or, rather, he wasn't a fan of things that lived in the dark.

His hands pushed aside shapes and objects. This one hard, that one soft. He worked through the hard objects until he found his tinderbox.

He opened it and set off a spray of sparks. They burned in his sight, bright flashes of white that lingered.

But he could see again, at least. Three flashes later and he had his candle lit.

He followed his trail through the sand back to the door, now just a part of the rock wall.

"That's fine. I've got what I want from you." He got to his feet, put on his pack, and set out for the ship.

The rest of the journey was uneventful, and he made good time.

"Where were you?" growled Captain Yardmorrow, brows drawn, and arms crossed.

"Almost got caught up in my work."

"You look like you've crawled in the dirt." Yardmorrow's eyes looked him over.

Raymond looked down too. In the light of the cavern, his poor state was revealed. All his clothes were covered in a light dusting of gray sand.

"It'll be good to get washed up then," Raymond said. His voice echoed in the much larger cavern, damped some by the water housing the *Sailfish*, the submarine he had hired to take him here.

Raymond walked by Yardmorrow, but then stopped and dug out his leather pouch. “Oh, one more thing. I’d like to settle up now.”

He tossed the chunk of gold. Yardmorrow caught it, then his eyes went big. “Will that do?”

Yardmorrow bit into it. “Welcome back, Mr. Ferris. It’s always a pleasure doing business with you.”

Eclectic Stories

Thank you for spending your precious time reading this book.

If stories make you salivate, learn more about lore, take an exclusive sneak peek behind the scenes, and get writing updates in my newsletter, Eric's Eclectic Stories.

As a bonus you'll get *Stories from the Deep*, a Patmos Sea Fantasy Adventure anthology that gives a glimpses of lore, extra prologues and epilogues, and character backstories.

If you aren't satisfied, unsubscribe at any time.

Join at erickercher.com.

-Eric Kercher

ALSO BY ERIC KERCHER

Patmos Sea Fantasy Adventure Series

Fathomless Pursuit | Architect's Prize | Ironbound Path
Sunken Prey – Unanswered Prophecy – Hardened Pilgrim – Final Peace

Seventh Hall Chronicles

Seventh Hall - Ode to the Survivors - Bastion of the Deep

Epic of Hornblood Castle

Siege of the Unfinished Keep – Winter at Hornblood – Branch of the Everlong

Castlebound Adventures

Rats in the Cellar!- Save the Cat!

Collections

Red Eagle Anthology | *Searchlight Anthology* | *Honeysuckle Nights*| *Ring of Calasia*

Stand Alone

Planet Reaping | *Dukedom Rumble* | *Savage Space Salvage* | *The Pioneer* | *Wrath of Wolfsbane*

About Author

Eric Kercher was born and raised in a small town on the Great Plains on good books. After attending a small state school on the east coast he joined the US Navy to serve his country and explore the world. He worked on submarines, and the world beneath the waves captivated him with all its mysteries and wonders. After spending time in larger cities, he's settled down in a quiet town with his wife and children. When not on an adventure in a good book the author enjoys creating dust woodworking, architecture, and spending time with loved ones.

Find out more at www.erickercher.com.

www.ingramcontent.com/pod-product-compliance
Lightning Source LLC
Chambersburg PA
CBHW030407020826
49168CB00022B/177

9781965871027